EARTHS

Written by Raskita Taylor

Illustrated by Ksenia Yulenkova - Ksuview

Earthy by Raskita Taylor
Illustrations by Ksenia Yulenkova - Ksuview
Text Copyright © 2022 Raskita Taylor
Illustrations Copyright © 2022 Ksenia Yulenkova - Ksuview

hearkenbooks.com

Dedicated to Aria & Ainsley, my two favorite humans.

Hello, my friend!
It is so lovely to see you here.
It is me, Earthy, your
favourite friendly sphere.

From Sydney to Rome to New York City, I have billions of people around.

There are mountain peaks, bubbling creeks, and many sights and sounds.

With all of these things,
I am not hard to see.

But people always seem to...

forget about me.

My favourite thing is the autumn breeze, where the leaves tickle and rustle with sound.

But as it seems, the leaves from
the trees are not the only
thing left on the ground.

It takes a winter's night when everything's right to see the glistening stars in the sky.

There are millions up here, and many fear that they will never be caught by your eye.

The world awakes with a breath of spring, and everything is reborn and new. Away goes the snow, the clouds, and the rain, leaving the sky all bright and blue.

Lately, the flowers have been fewer and fewer, and the bees are harder to see. The flowers and trees miss their company, and everything seems less green.

Beaches and boat rides and riverside walks, the summer brings the sun! With sparkly sand and ice cream in hand, it is hard not to have fun.

But my fish friends are
left crowded by things other than
the sand. Too many things are being washed
into their homes, like rubbish from the land.

I have been around for billions of years and have had many things call me home. From mighty dinosaurs to tiny bugs and things that crawl, fly, and roam.

I have loved every creature, plant, and all that has kept me company here, especially my human friends, whom I have always held so dear.

I have seen their brilliance, felt their cries, and cheered for them and their dreams. But I now have a wish, an ask of them, to see if we can work as a team.

If we work together to help each other clean up
and care for this dome. We can make this
place a better place for everyone
who calls me their home.

Every piece of litter we pick up
or flower we plant will help
along the way.

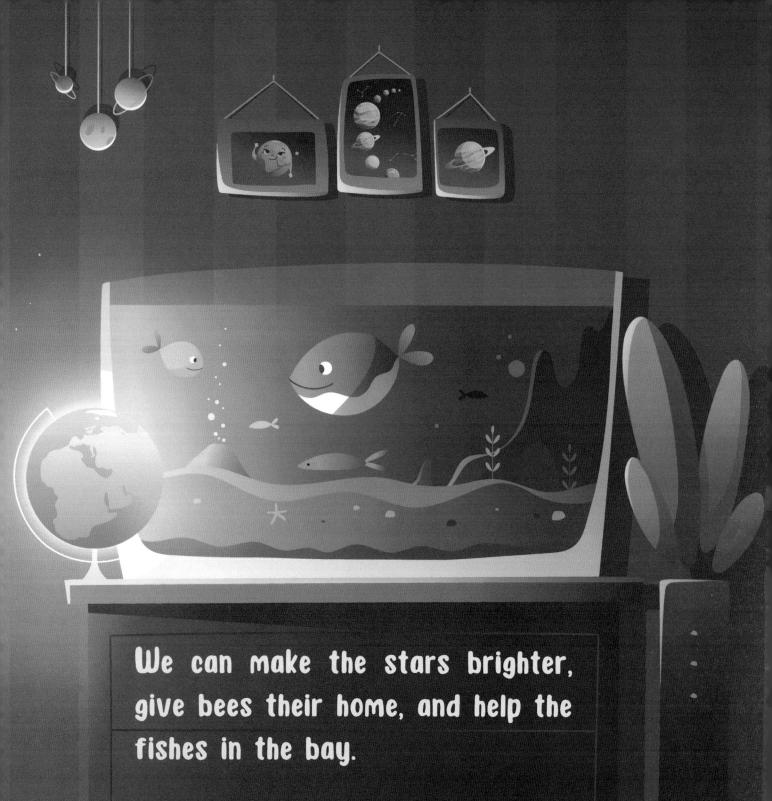

We can make the stars brighter,
give bees their home, and help the
fishes in the bay.

Together we live in this beautiful place and can help make it better each day.

I long to be the best planet I can be, but
I was hoping you could help me along the way.

Things you can do to help:
Plant trees & flowers

Save water & electricity

Walk or bike more often

Pick up litter & recycle

Printed in Great Britain
by Amazon